Halloween

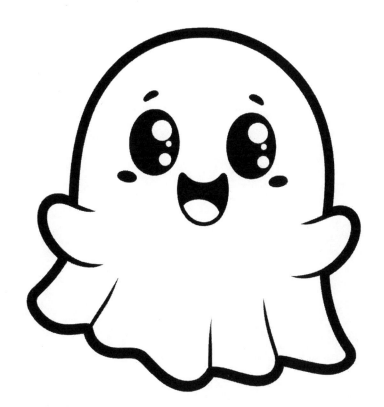

Coloring Book for Kids

Happy Halloween

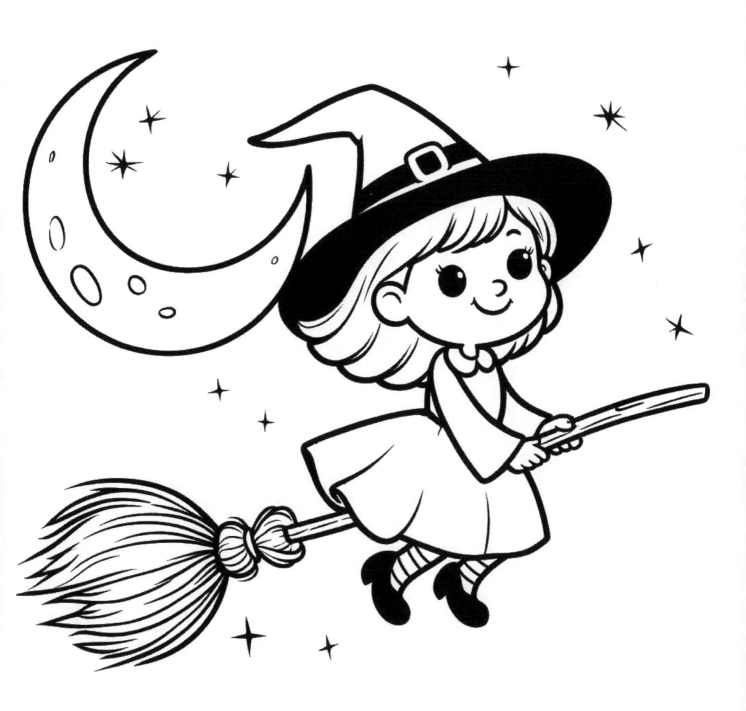

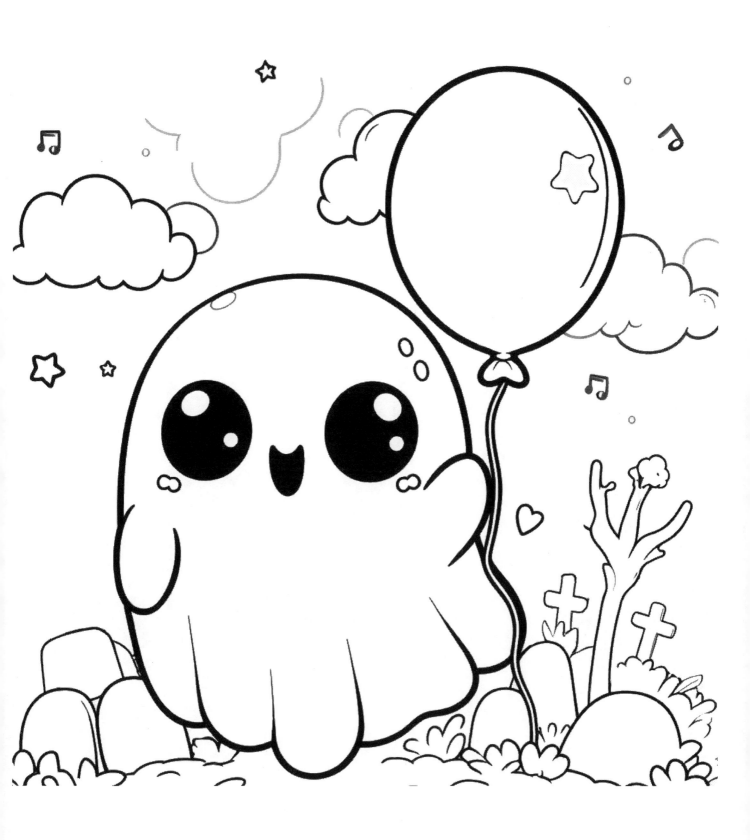

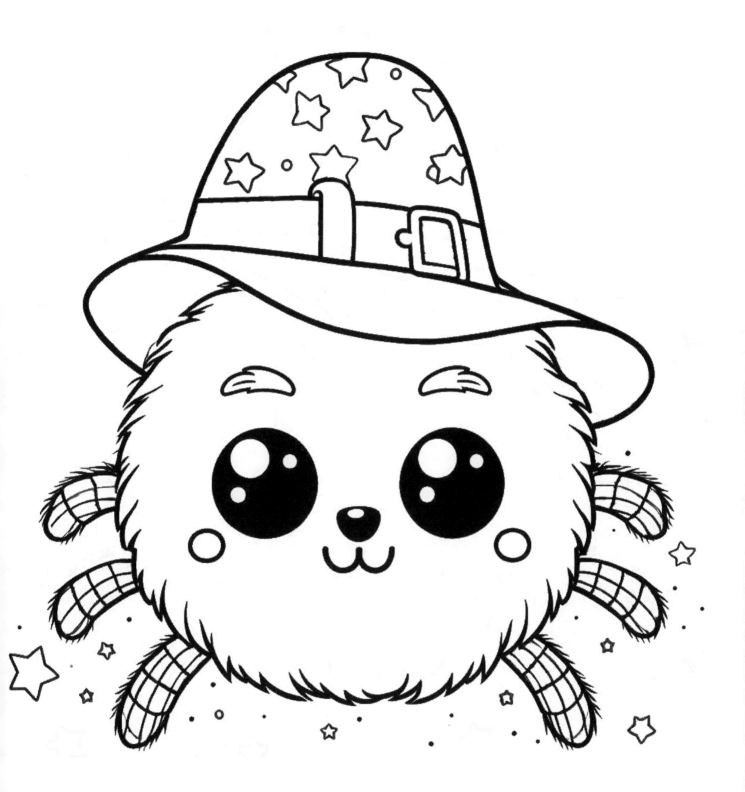

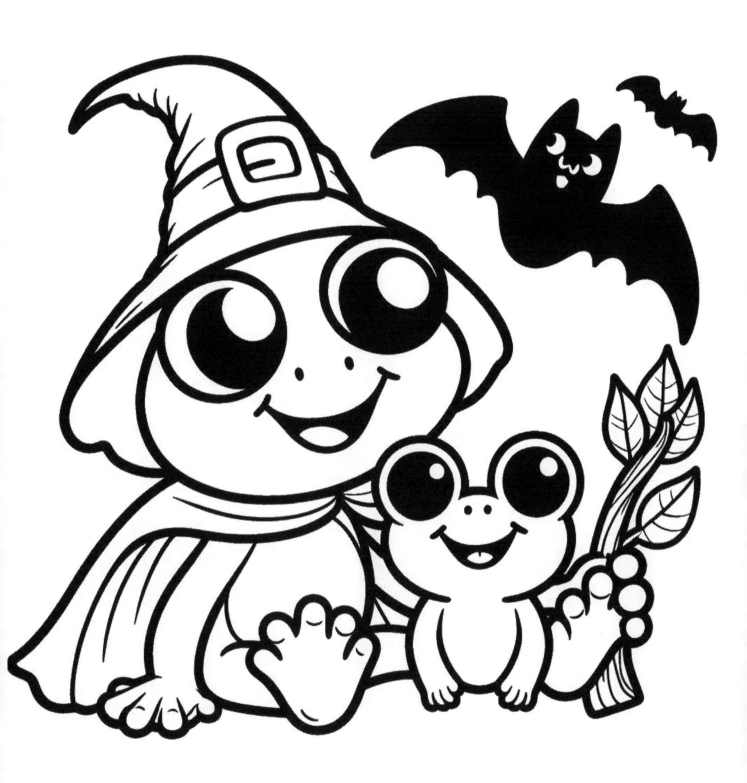

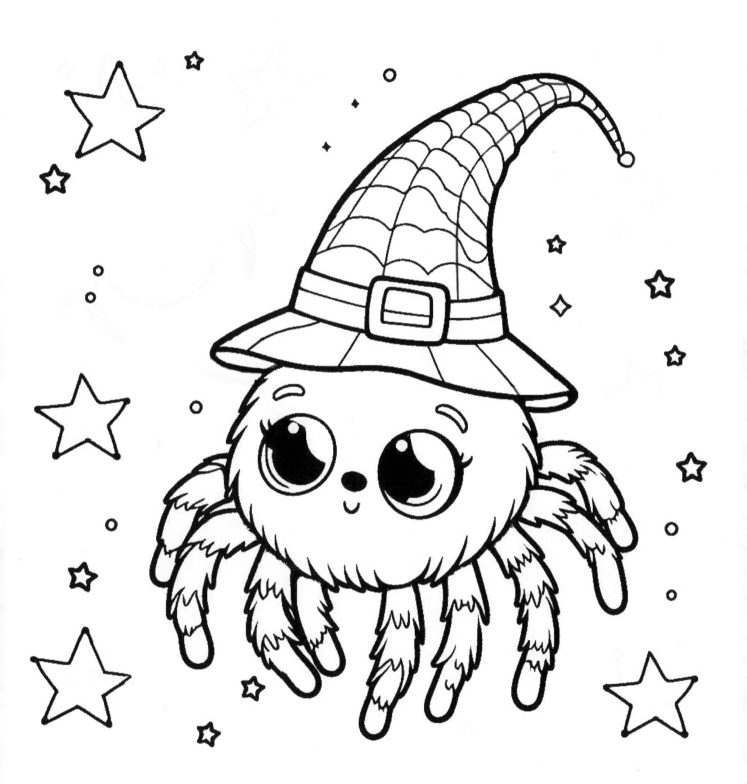

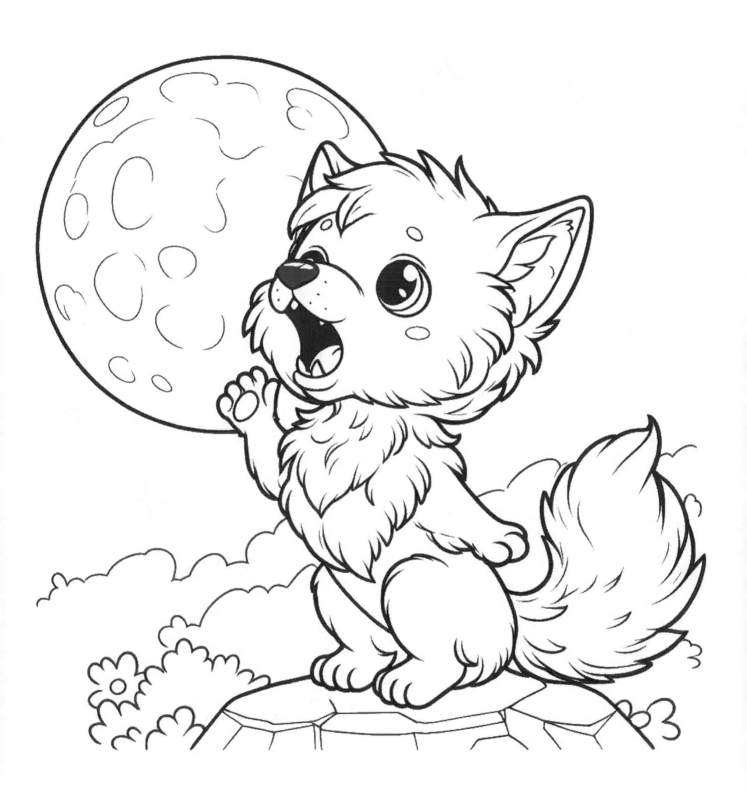

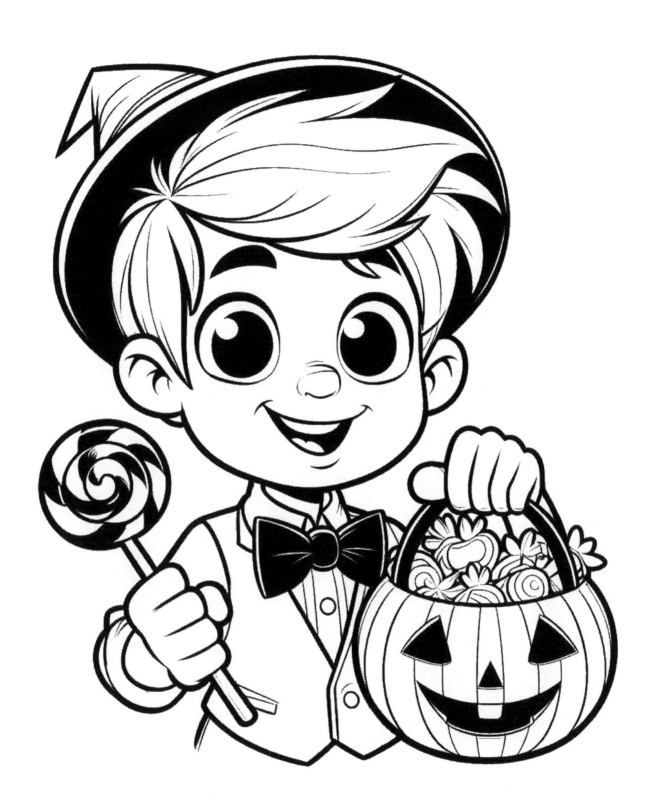

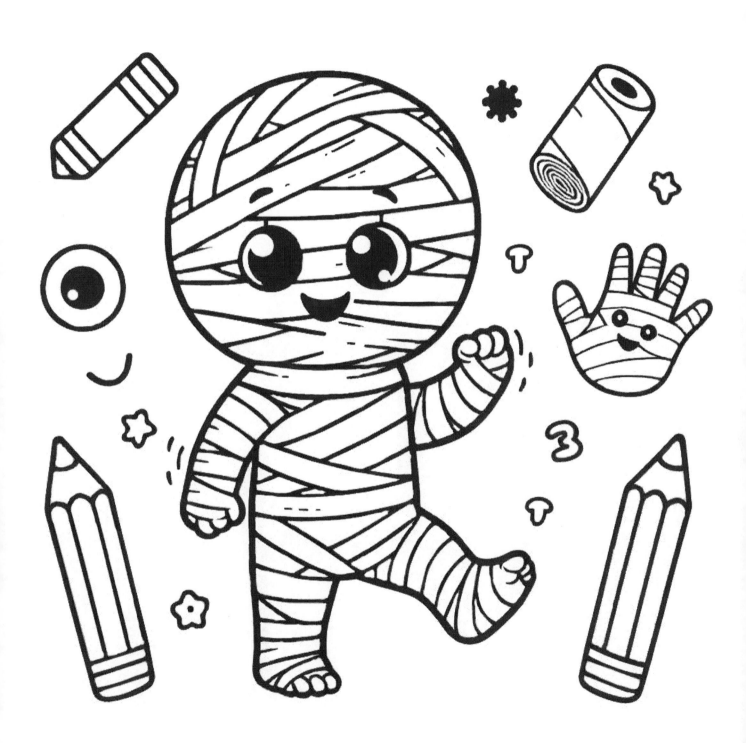

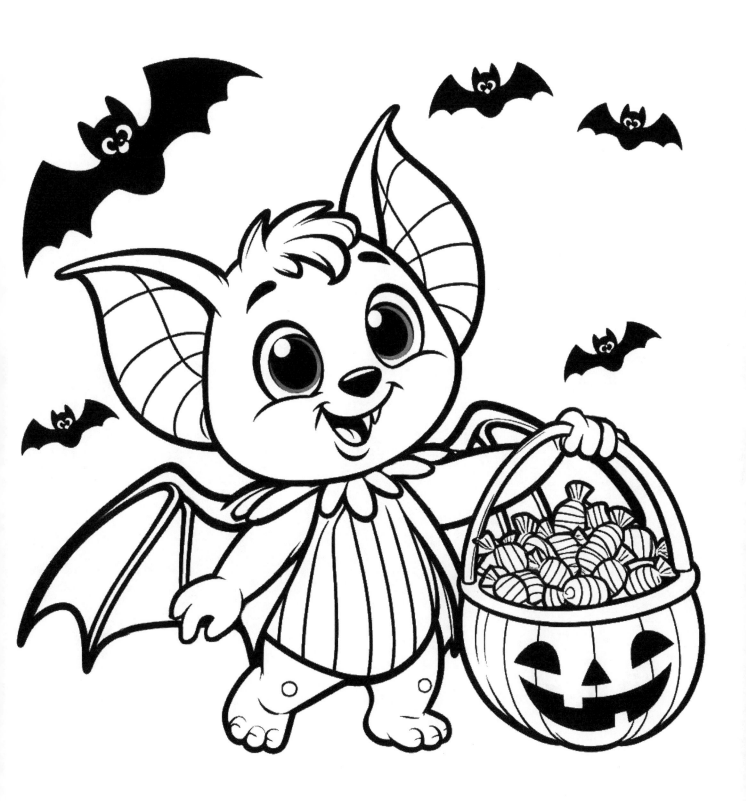

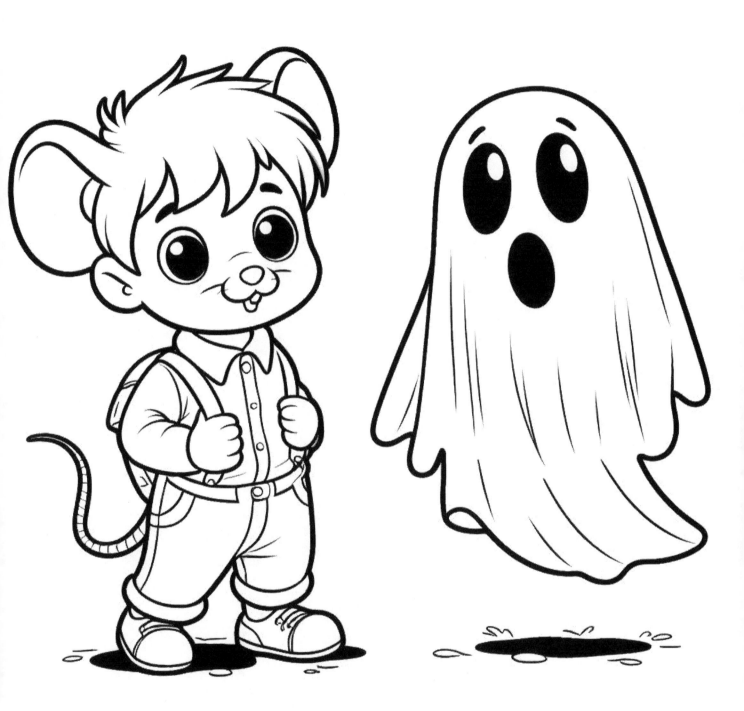

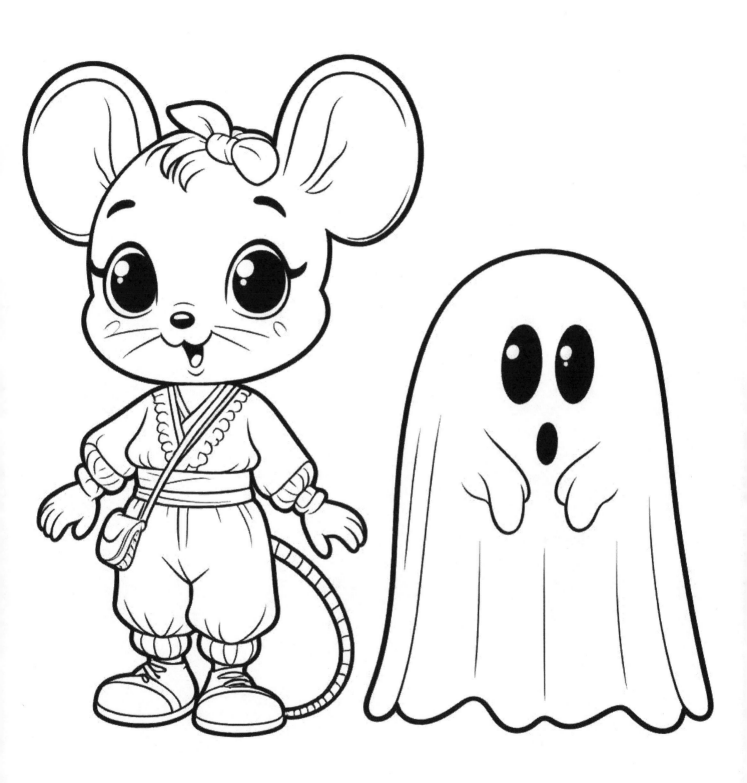

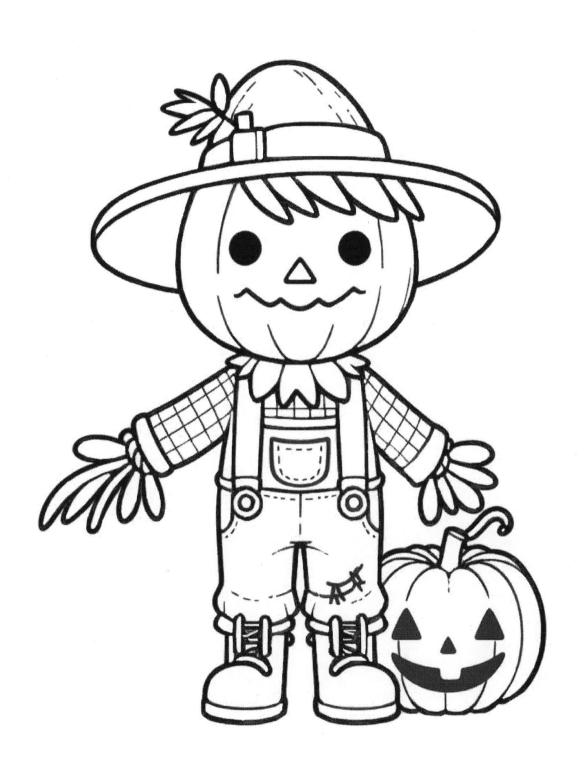

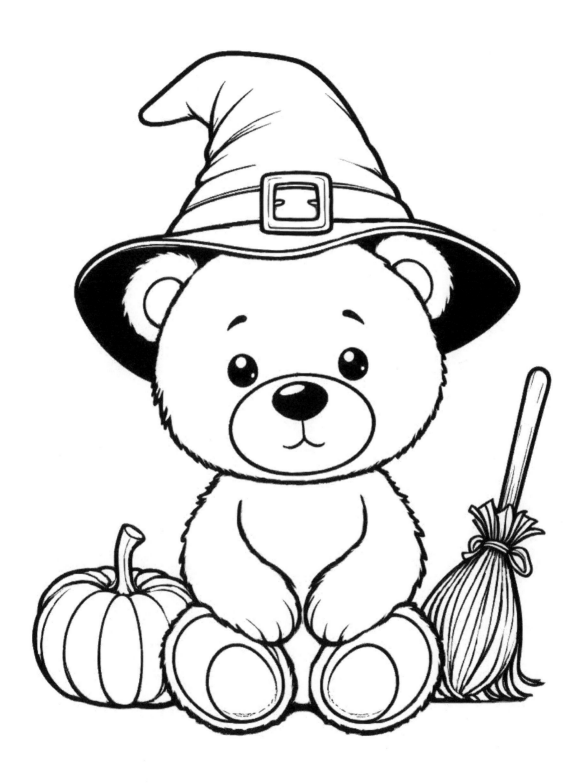

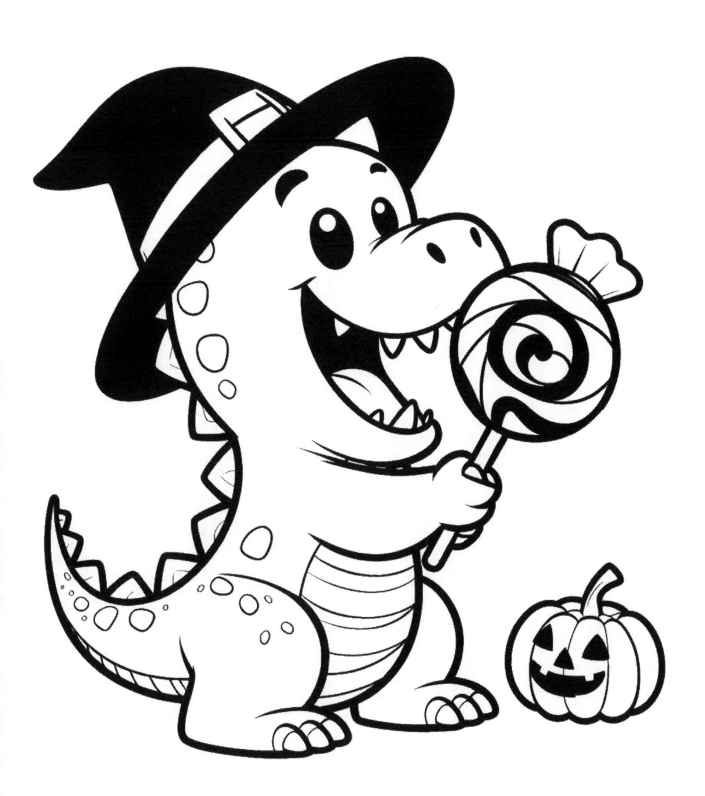

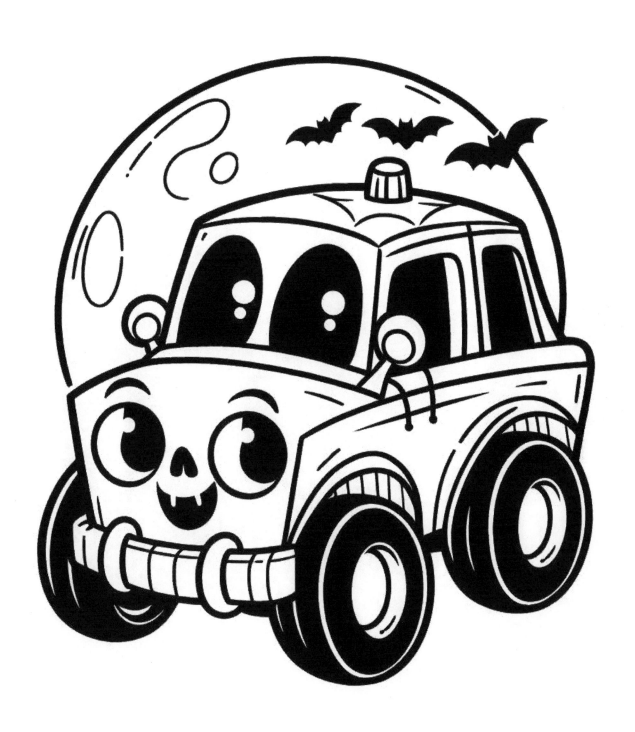

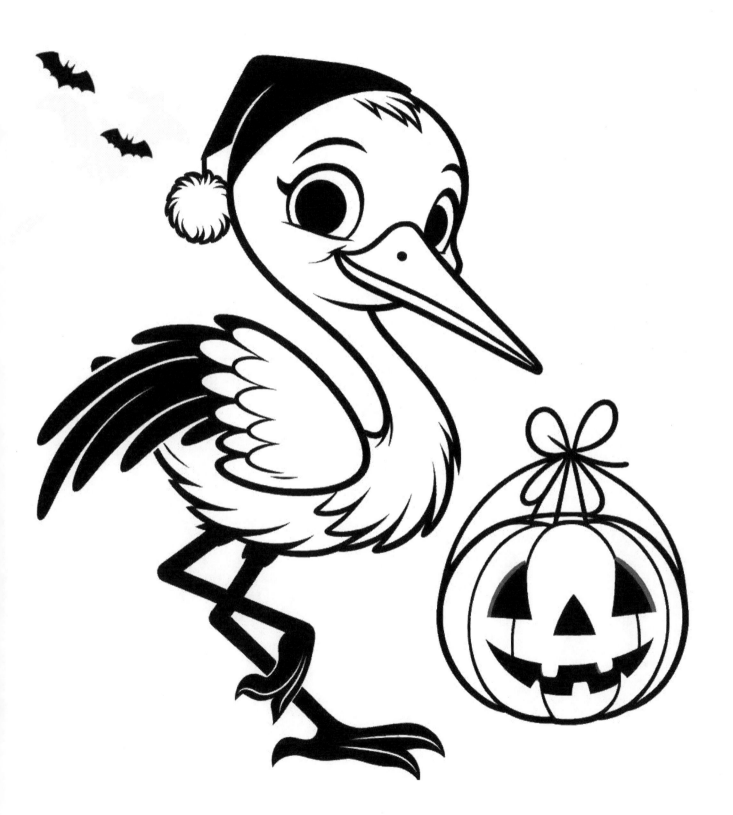

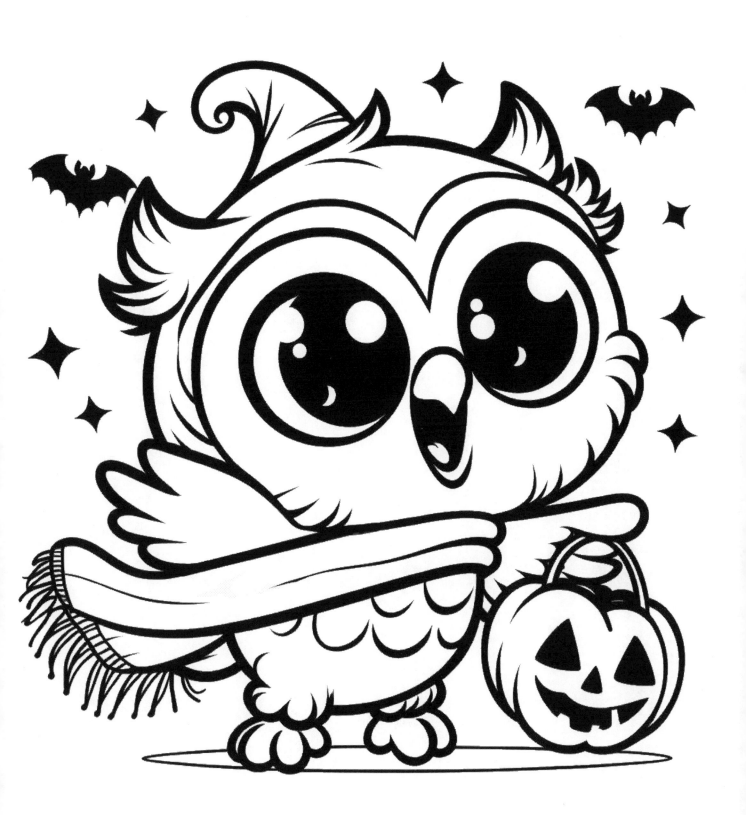

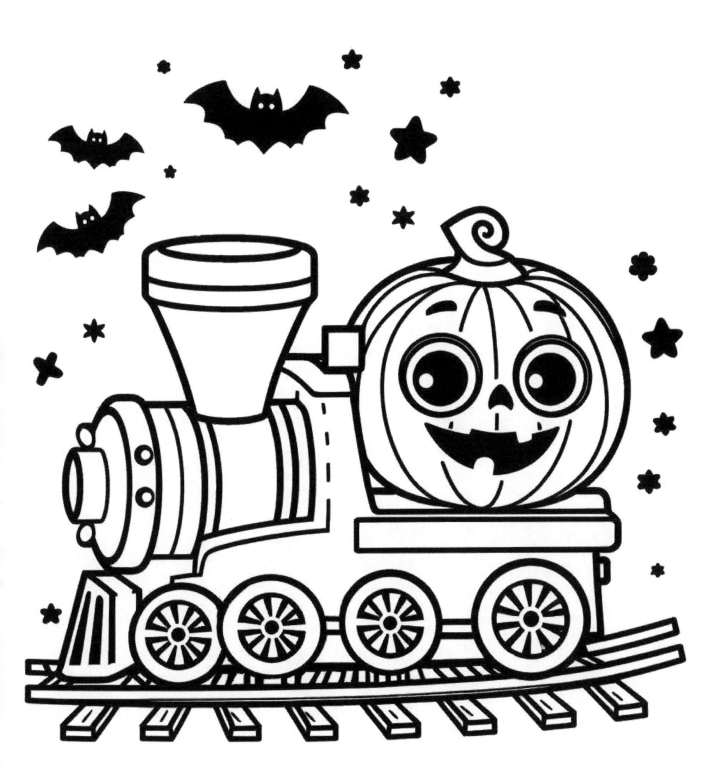

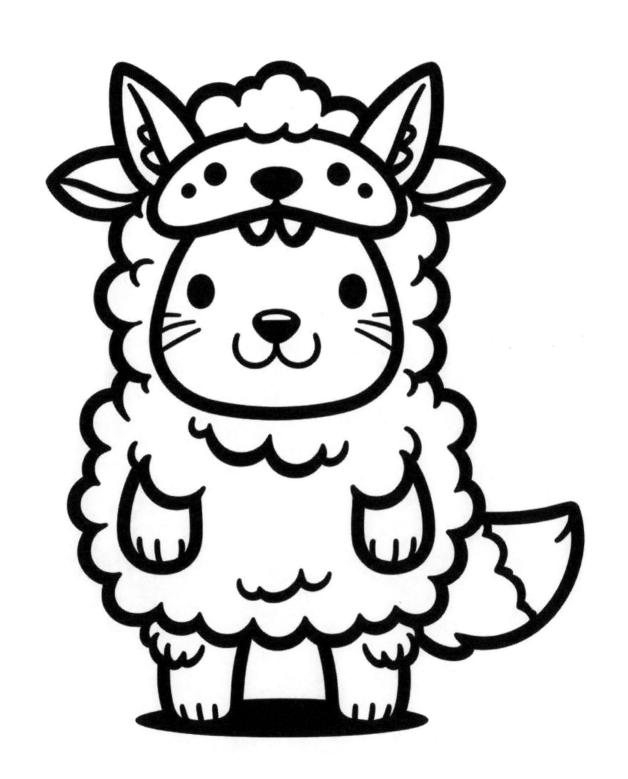

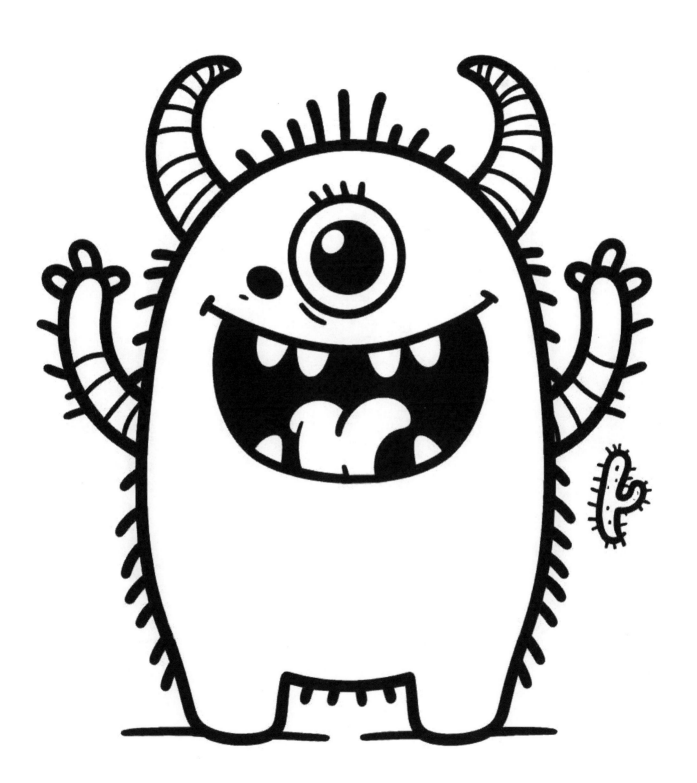

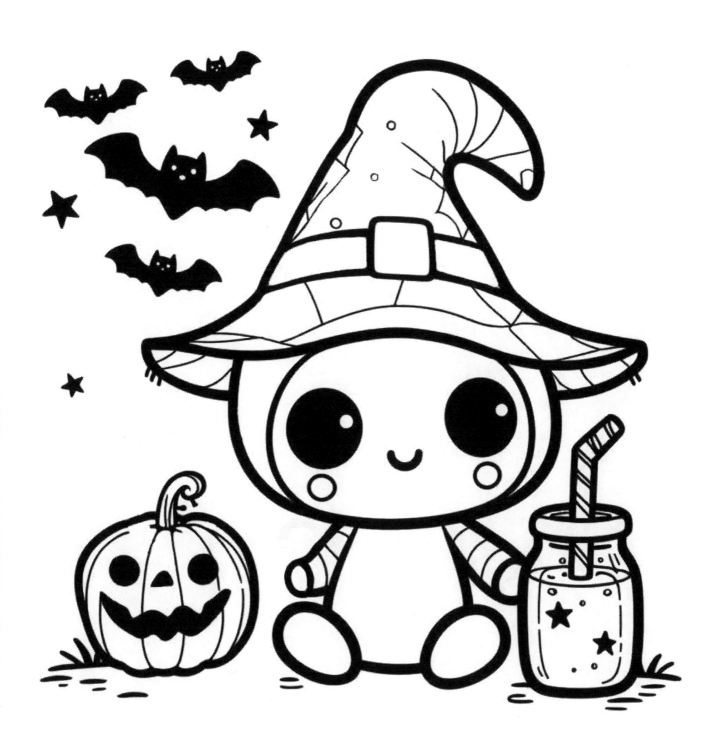

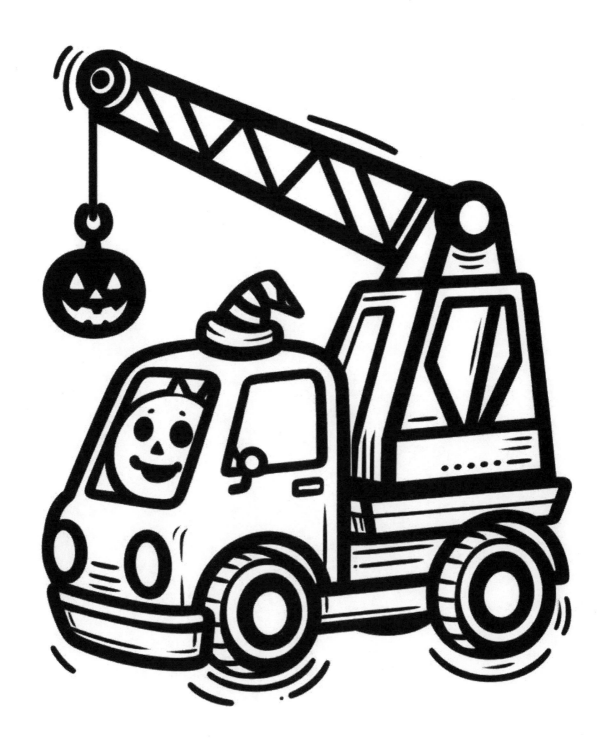

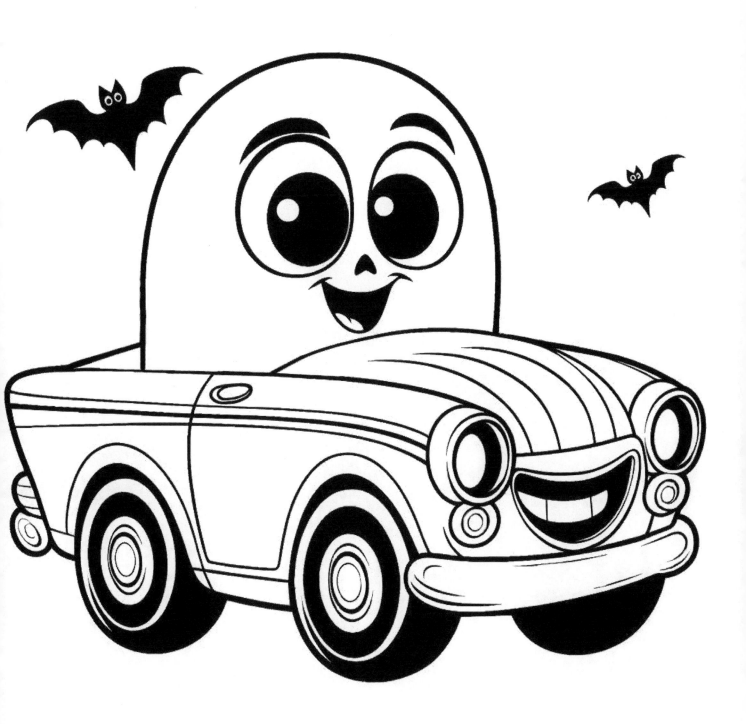

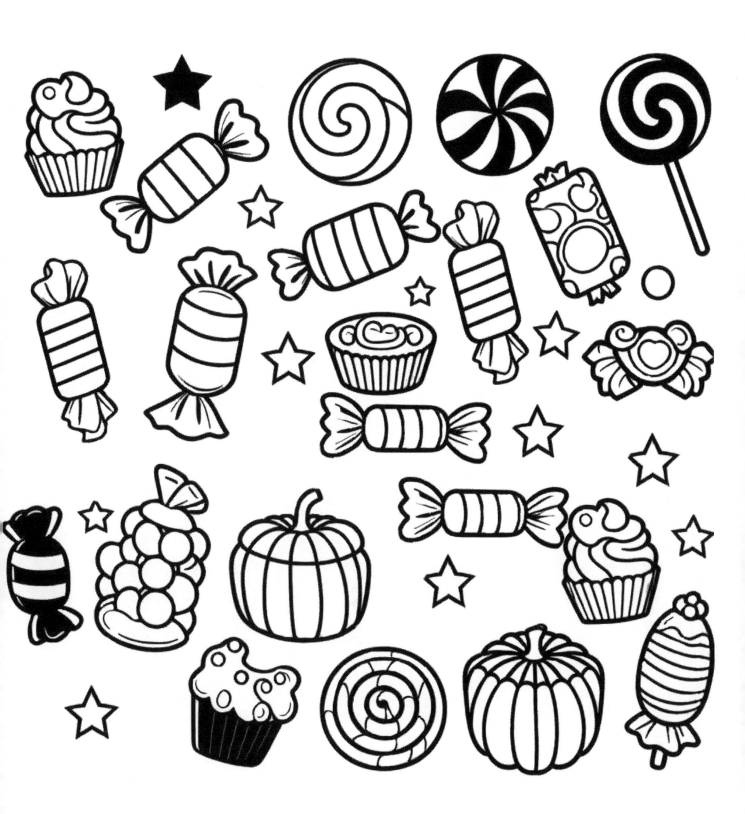

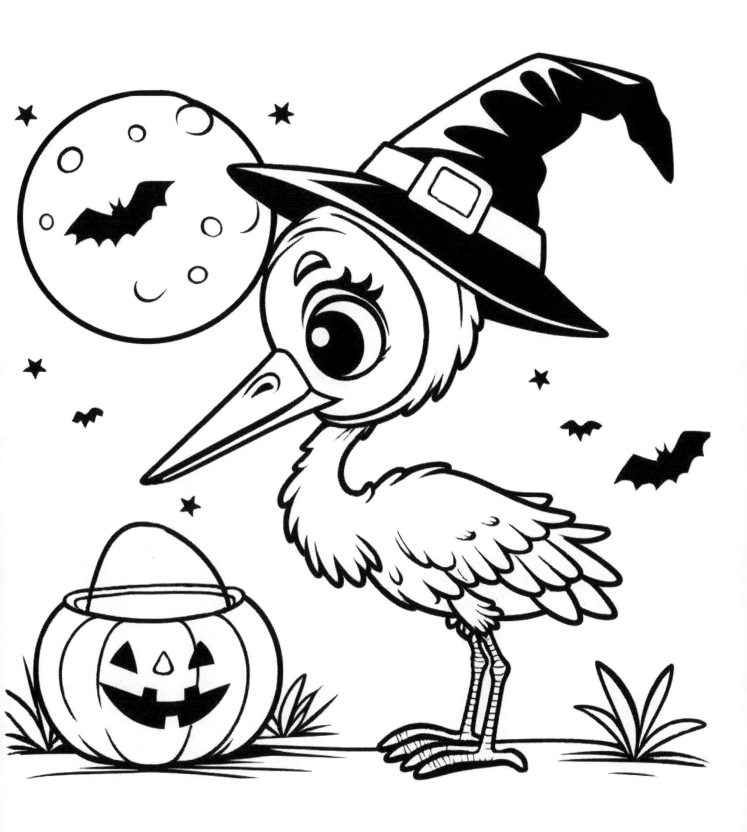

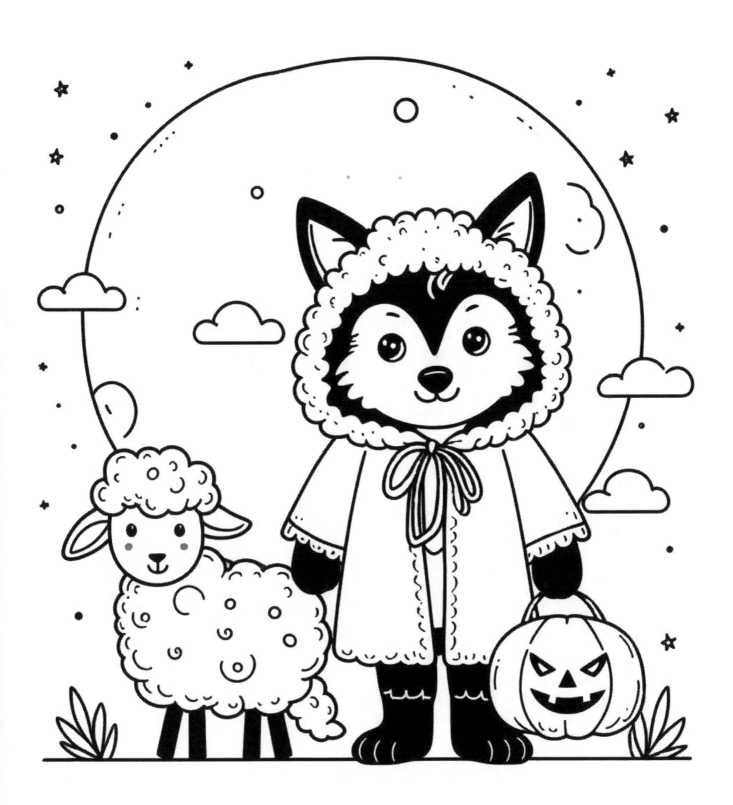

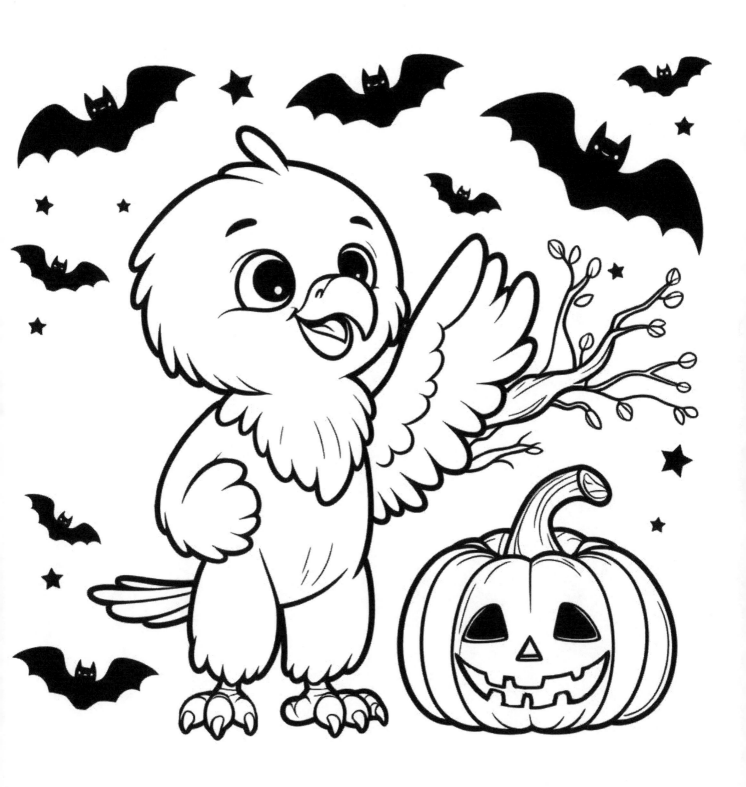

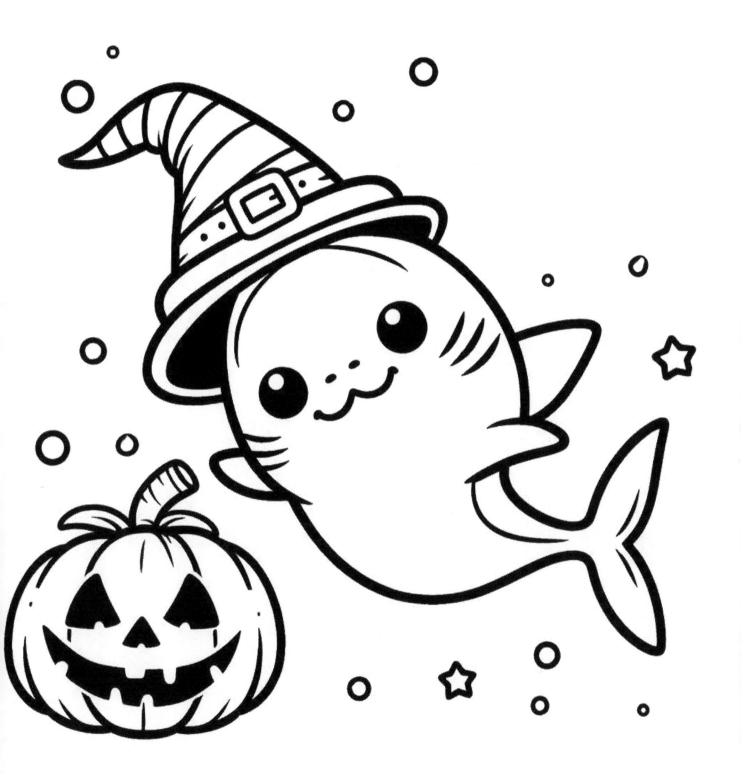

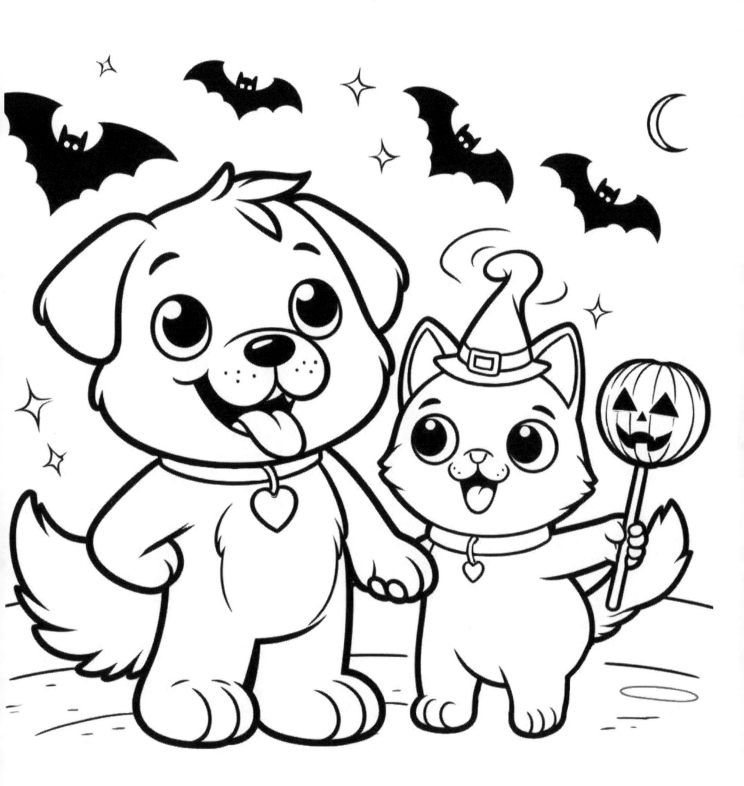

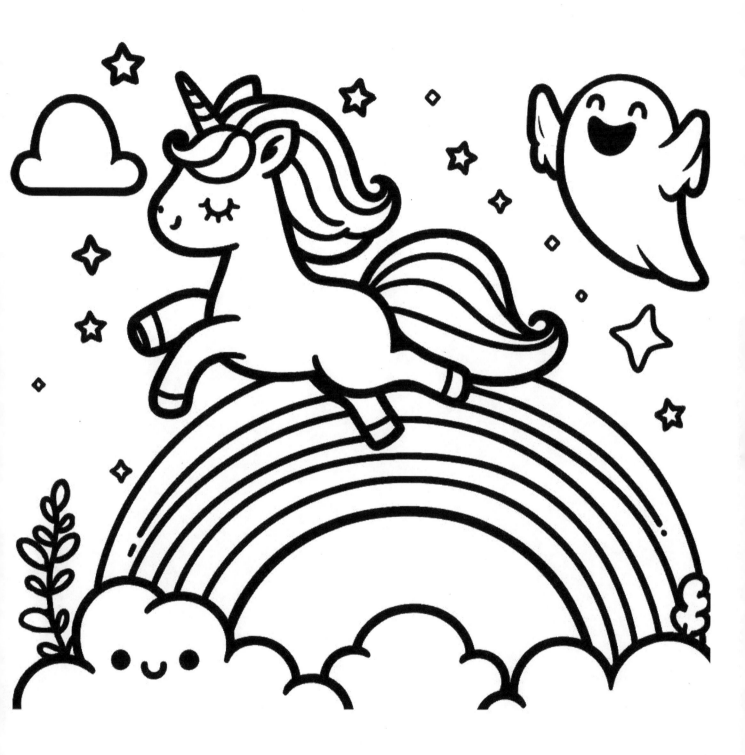

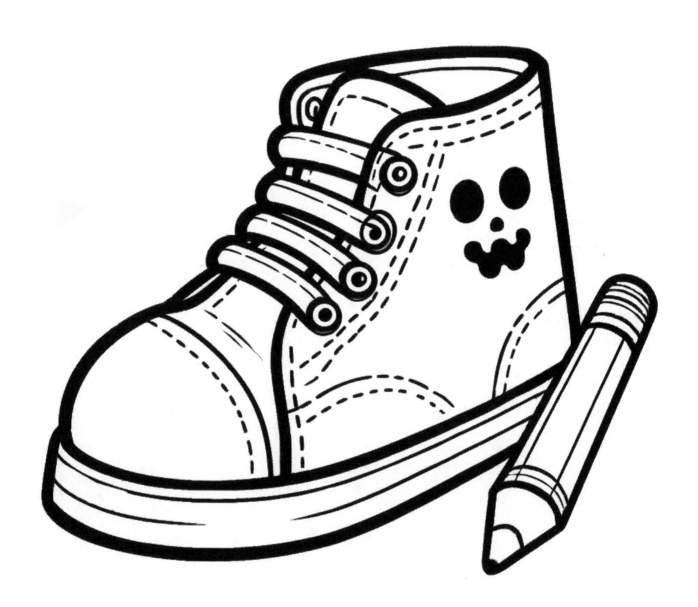

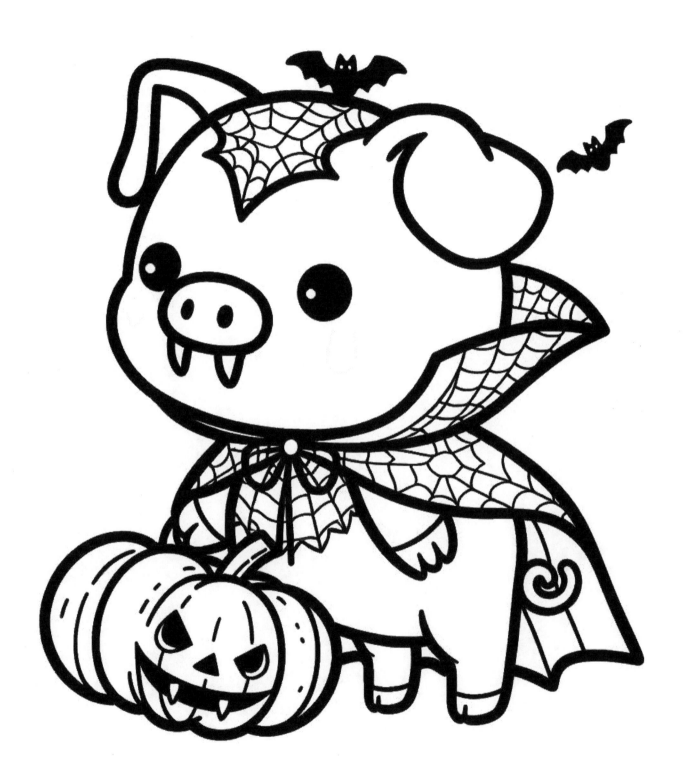

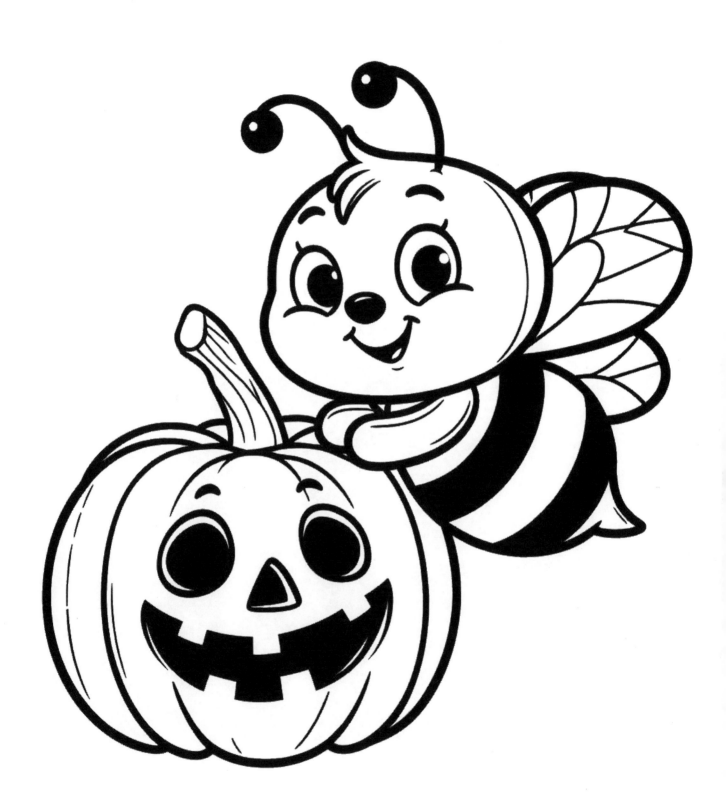

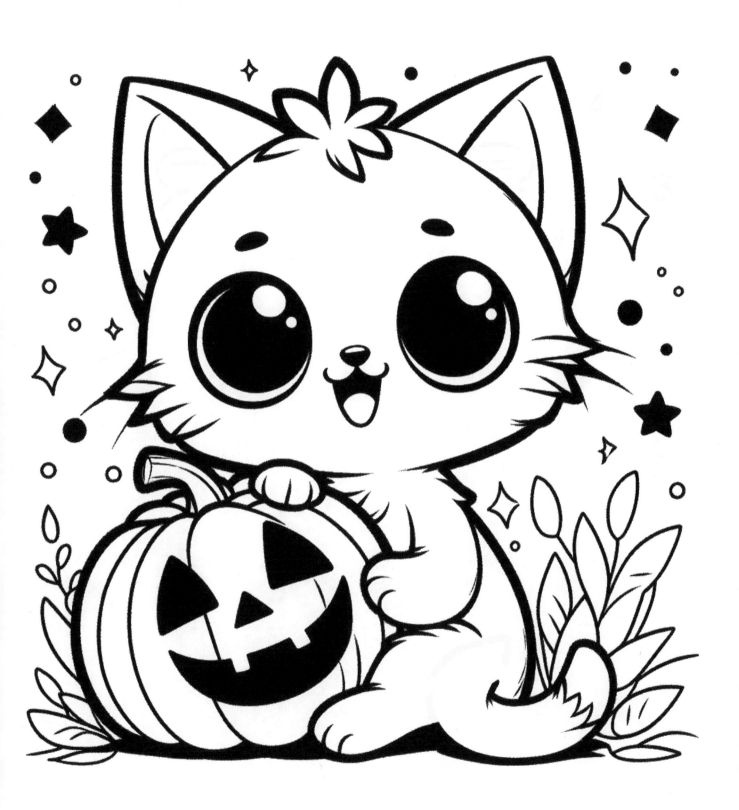

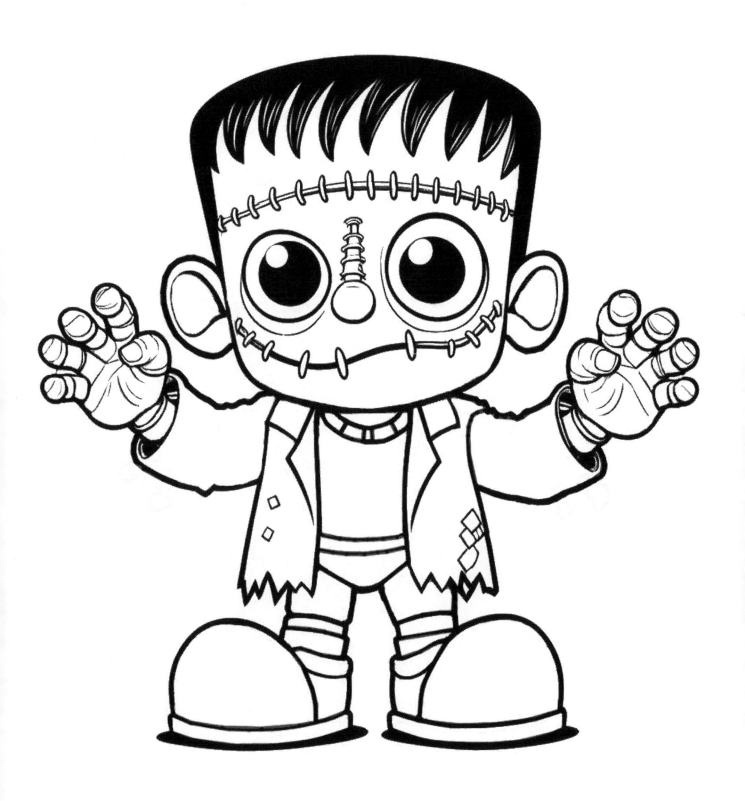

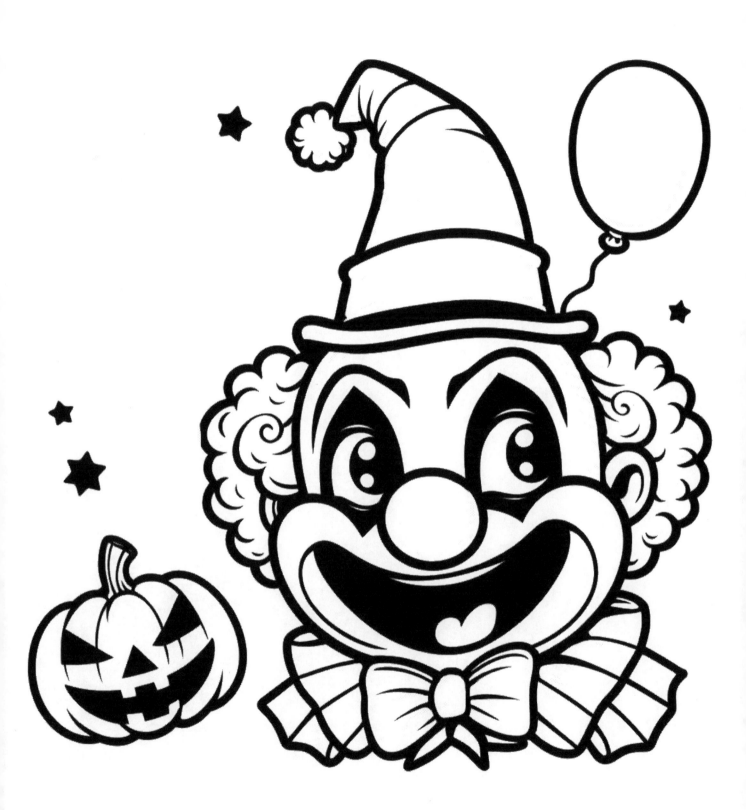

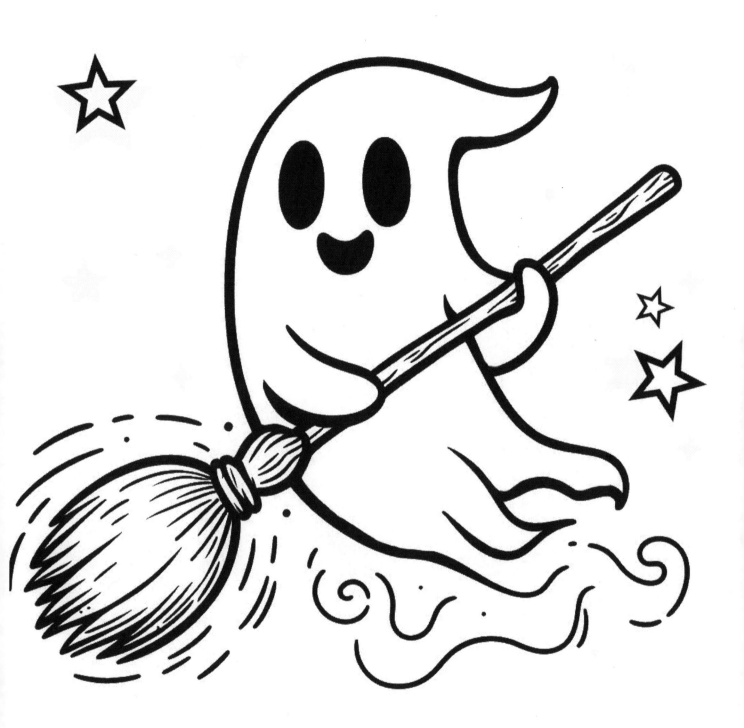

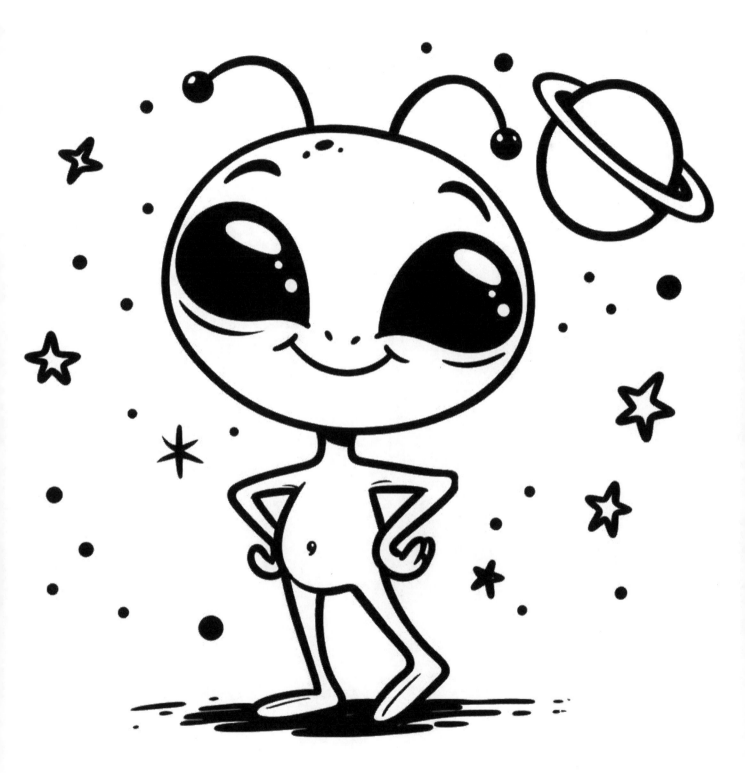

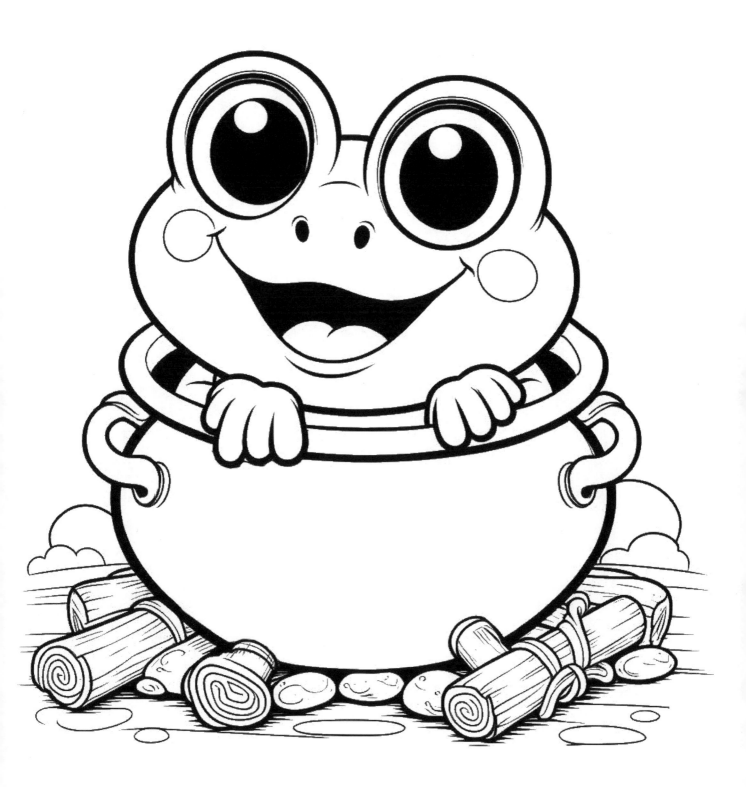

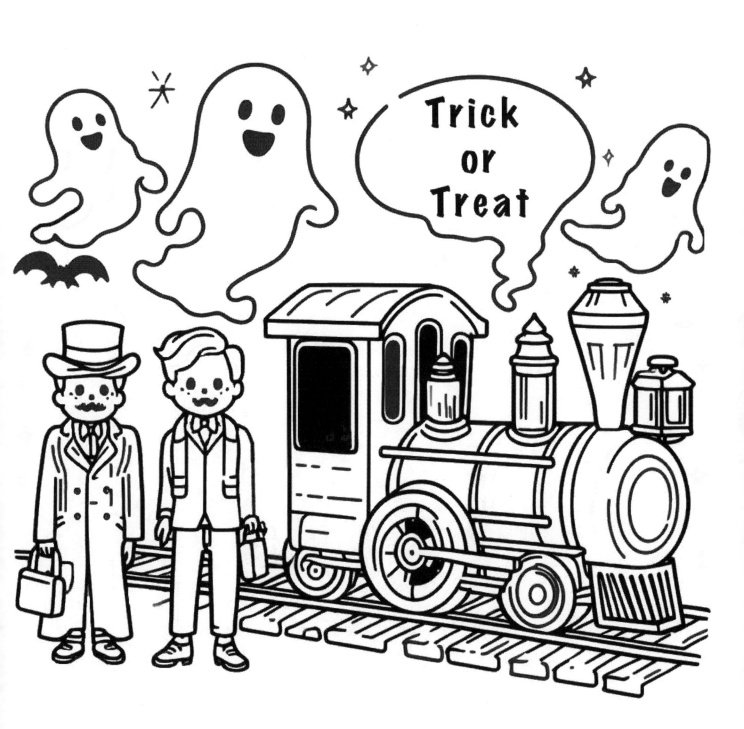

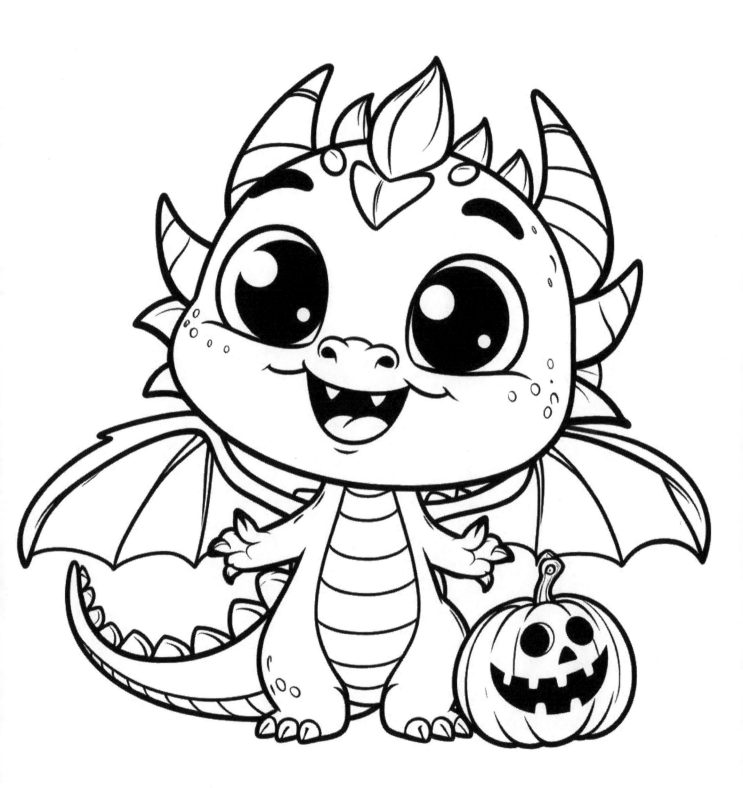

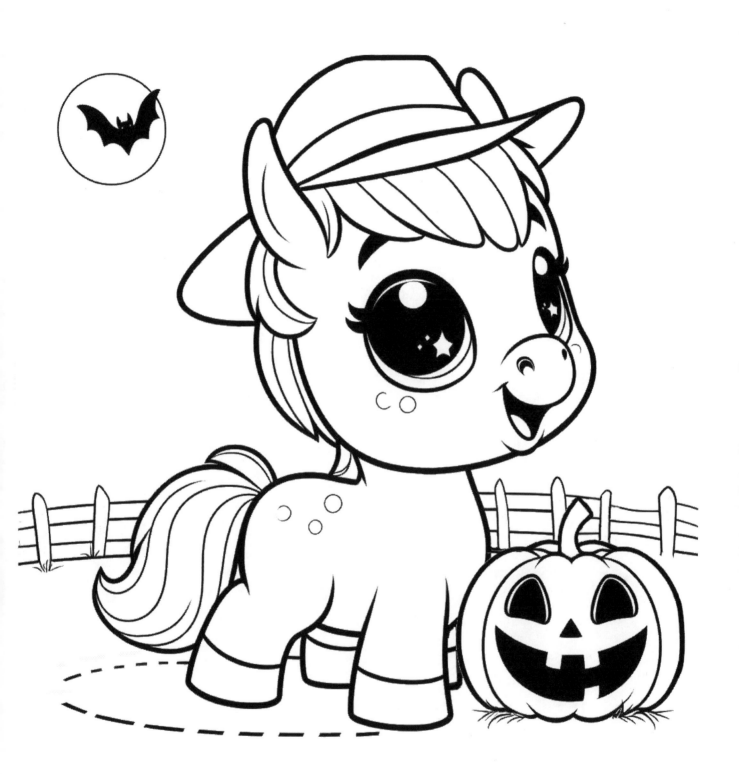

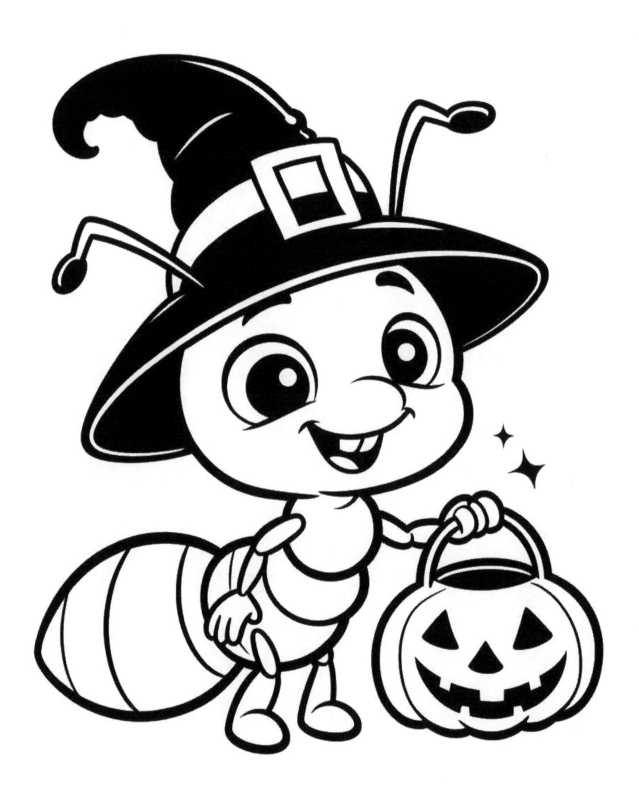

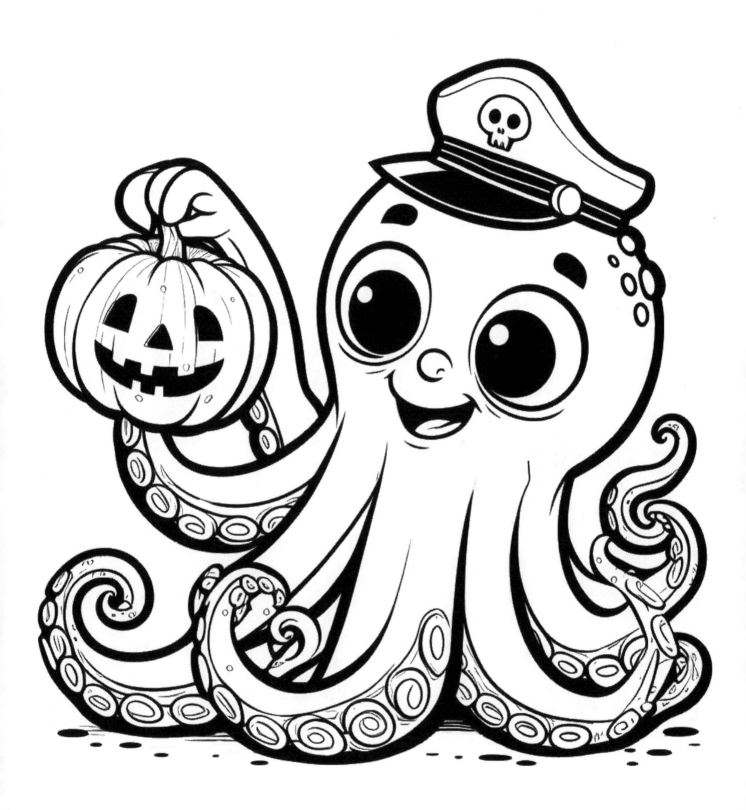

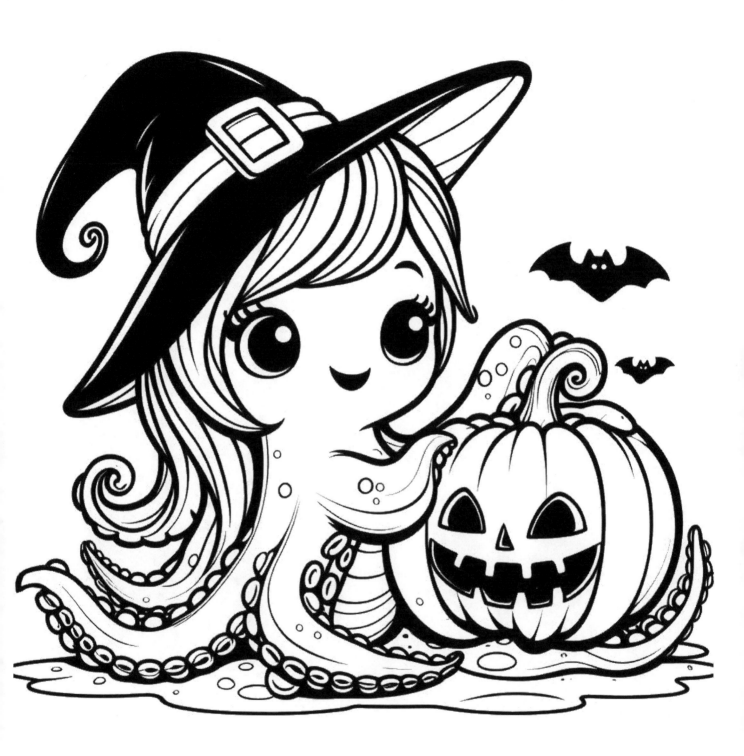

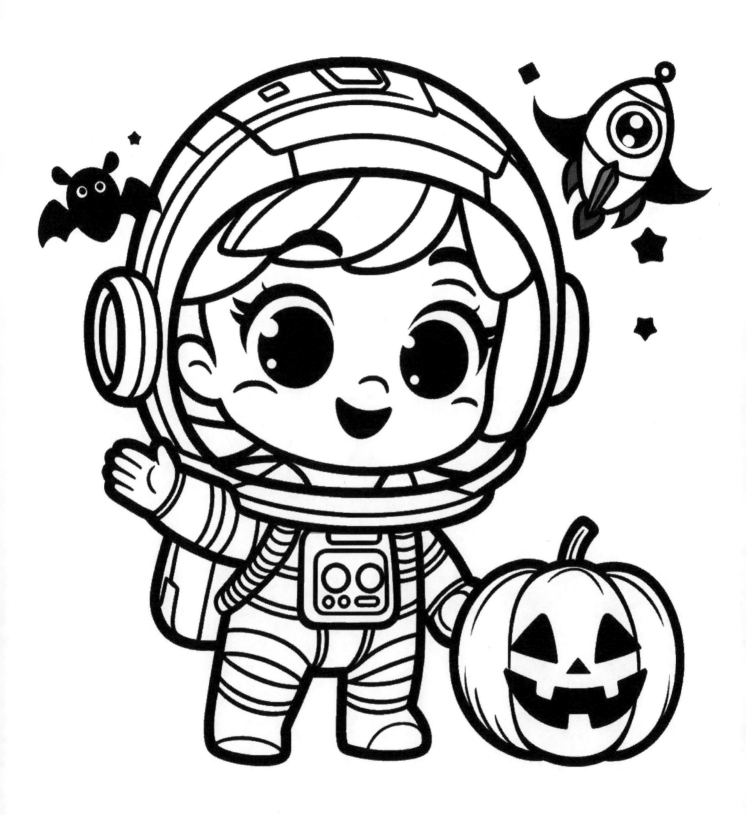

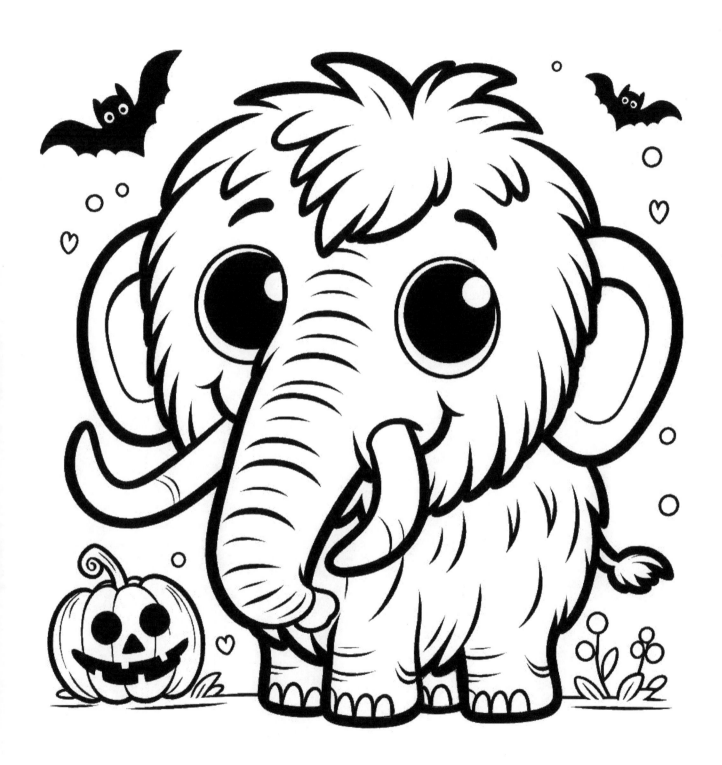

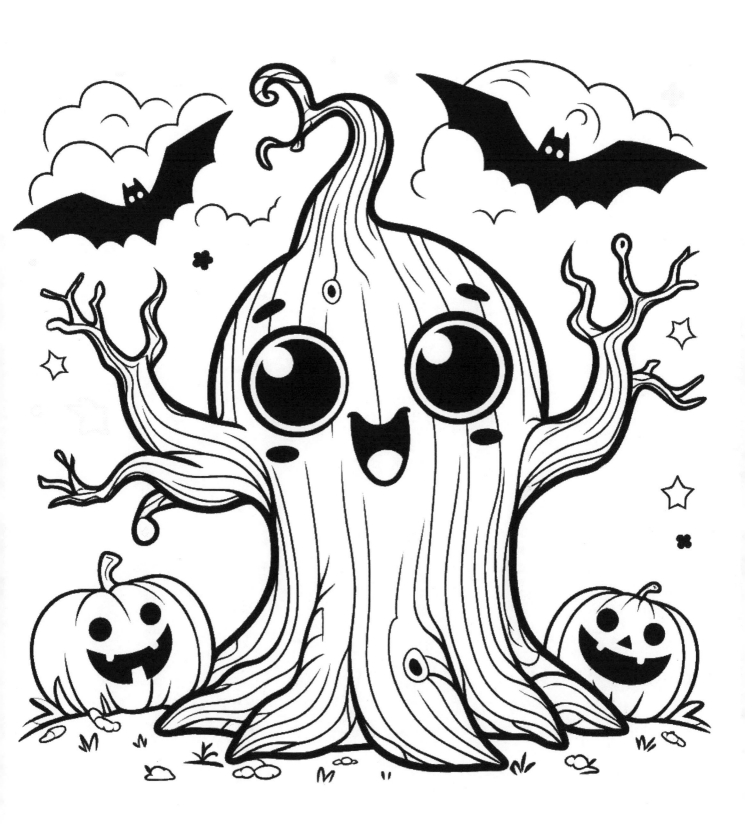

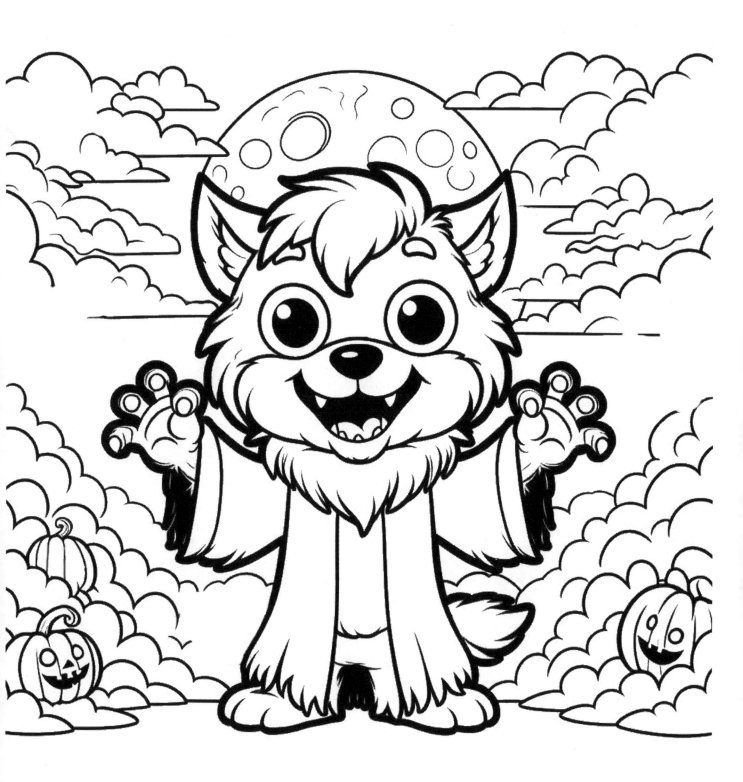

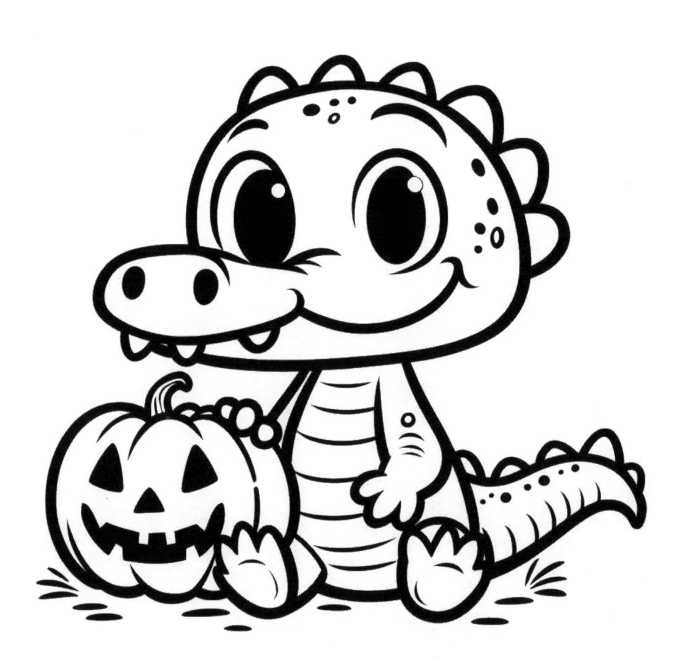

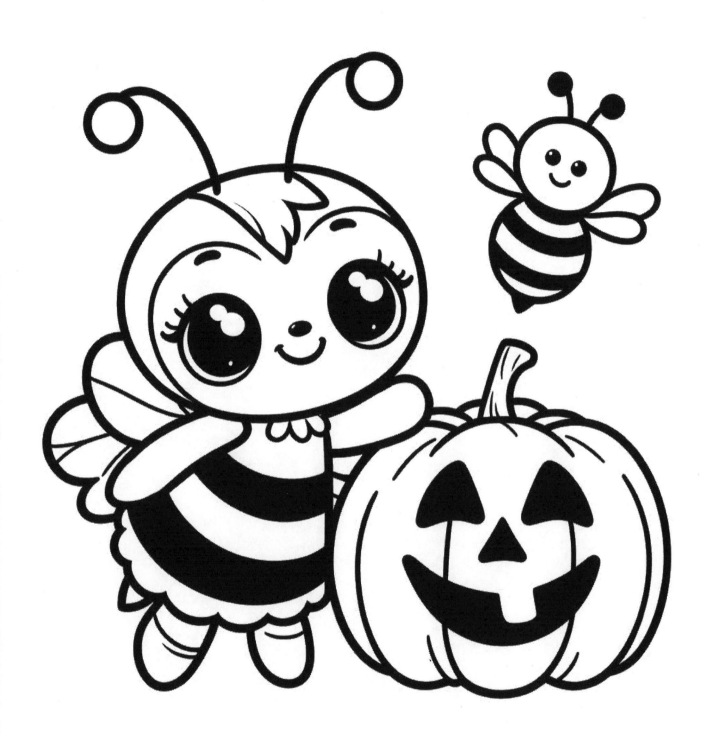

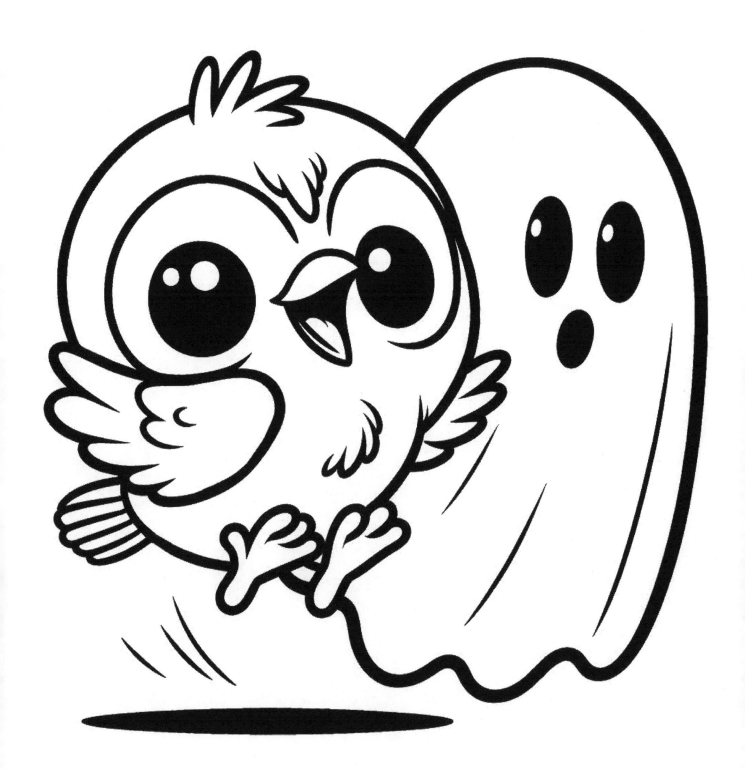

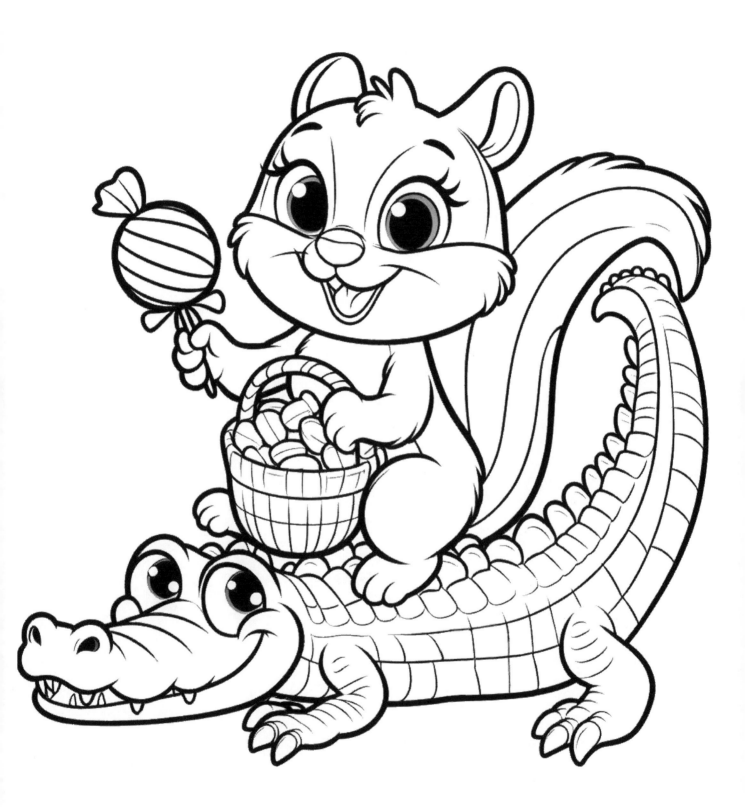

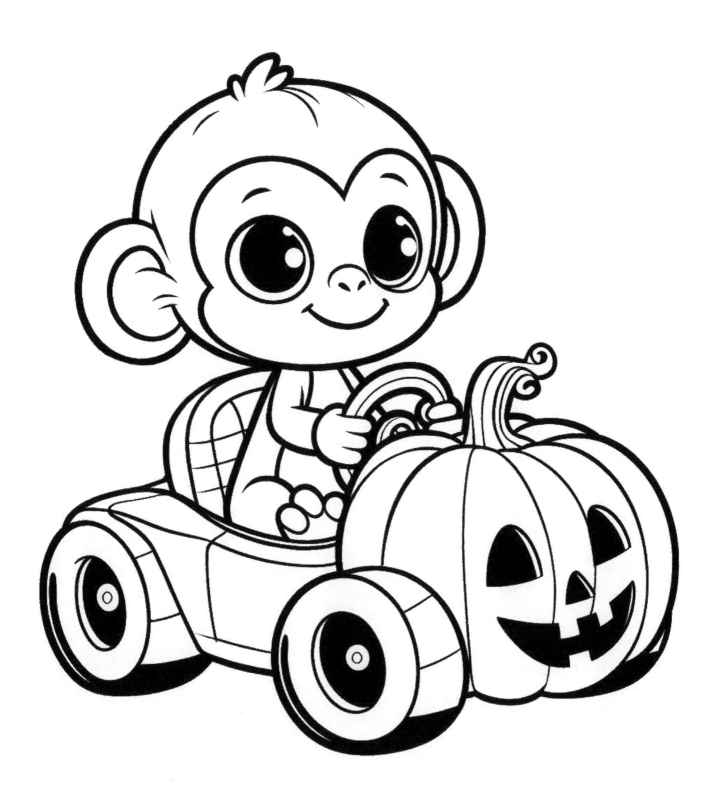

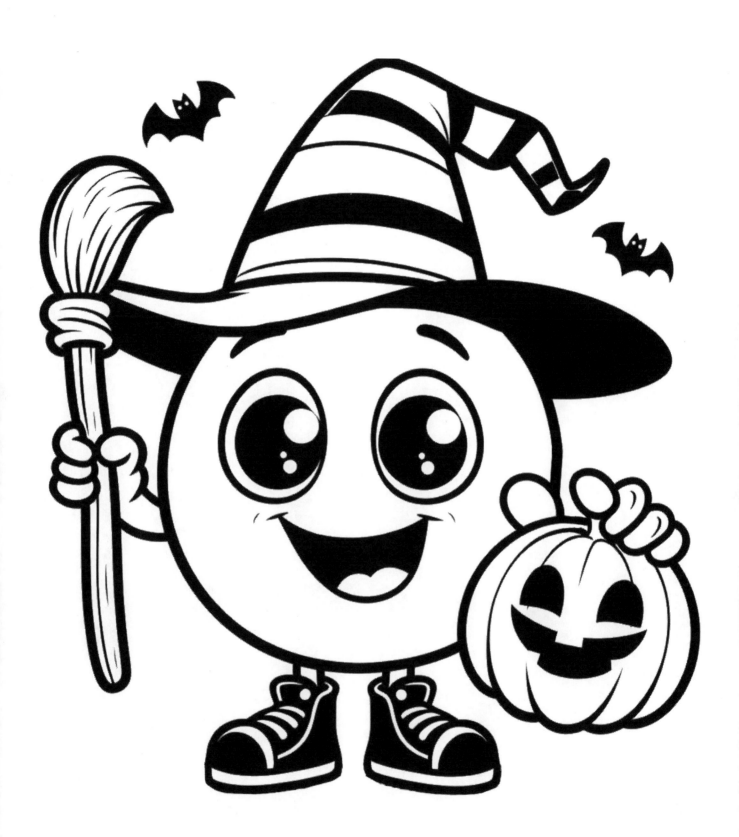

Connect the dots to create an image and then color it.

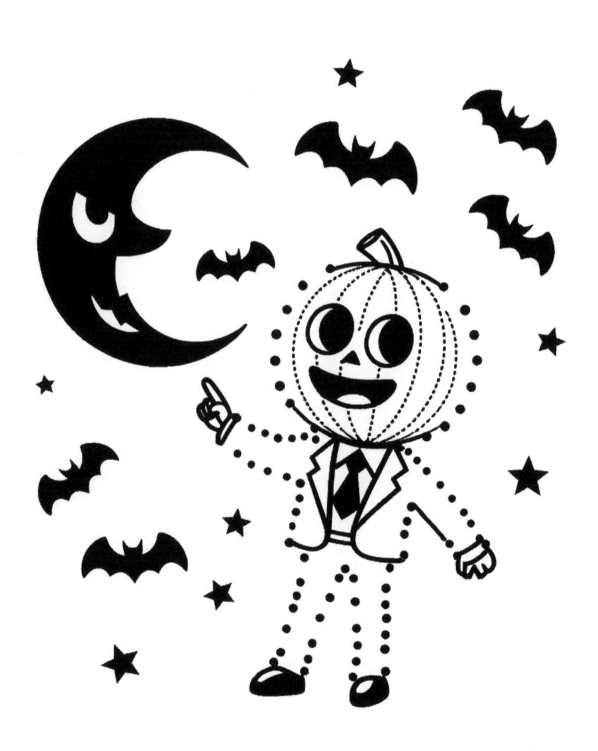

Help the witch find the path to her broom.

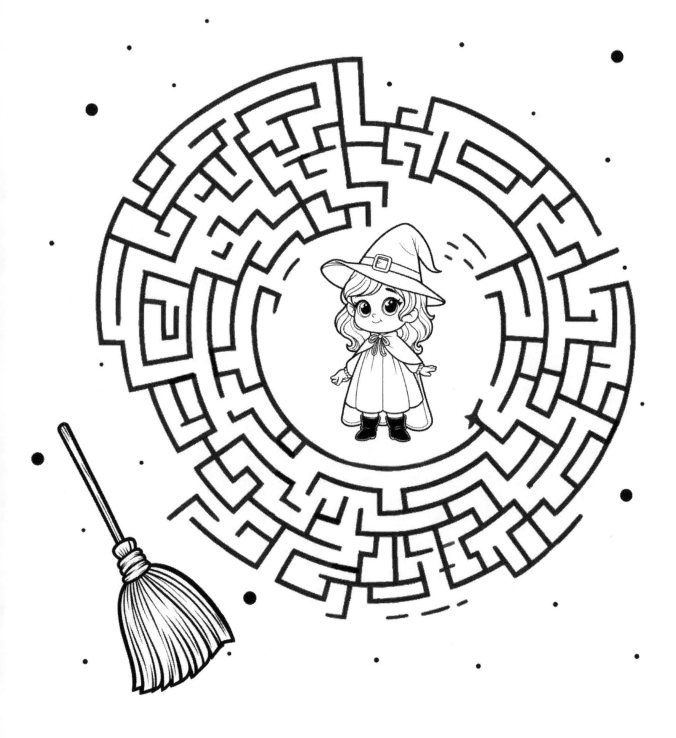

There are 5 differences between the pair of images.

See how many you can find.

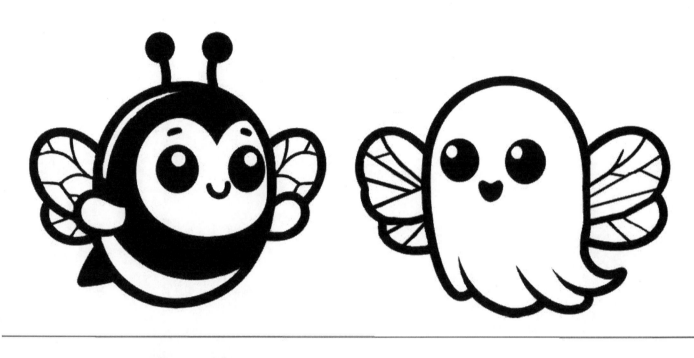

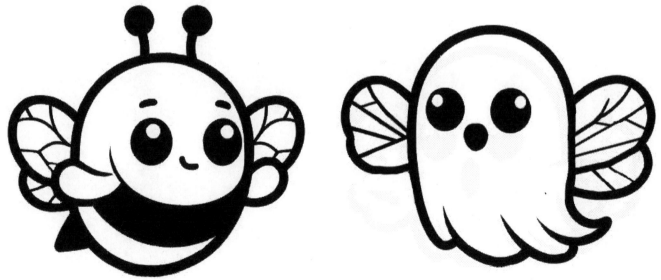